In the field

How many cabbages
can you count?

Seeds

Trowel

Rabbit

Pumpkin

Carrot

Cabbage

How many butterflies can you see?

Which vegetable is the biggest?

SEEDS

Corn

Shovel

Wheelbarrow

Scarecrow

Can you spot the caterpillar?

In the meadow

Can you spot the hidden rabbit?

Cow Calf Sheep Lamb Shepherd Puddle

How many birds can you count?

Which sheep is dirty?

Bird

Butterfly

Sheepdog

Hedge

Can you spot the deer?

In the stables

What noise does a horse make?

How many horses can you count?

Horse	Foal	Saddle	Apple	Flies	Reins

What does a vet do?

Horseshoe

Vet

Brush

Broom

Can you spot the mouse?

In the barn

What animal is in the barn window?

Water trough Food trough Hay Donkey Goat Goose

How many baby goslings are there?

Which path leads the goose back to the pond?

Gosling

Turkey

Ladder

Rooster

Can you spot the spider?

Working the land

Can you spot the differences between the two sheep?

Tractor

Trailer

Wheel

Combine harvester

Potato

Hay baler

What noise does a cow make?

Which animals are in the trailer?

Bale stacker

Lawn mower

Potato planter

Hat

Can you spot the wasp?

In the coop

What can you see in the sky?

Which path leads the chick back to the coop?

Eggs

Chicken

Chick

Worm

Cat

How many chicks
can you count?

Bowl

Rat

Sun

Rainbow

Can you spot
the feather?

In the orchard

How many trees can you count?

Peach Plum Pear Cherry Basket Gloves

Who is picking the pears?

How many cherries are on the ground?

Crate

Leaf

Tree

Bush

Can you spot the snail?

In the pond

Can you jump like a frog?

Frog **Duck** **Duckling** **Reeds** **Lily pad** **Rocks**

How many lily pads does the duck family have to cross to get to the other side?

What type of weather can you see?

Dragonfly Squirrel Cloud Swan

Can you spot the fish?

In the farmyard

Is the bucket
full or empty?

 Bee

 Beehive

 Rake

 Well

 **Bucket**

 Birdbath

What animal is in the field?

Who has a woolly coat?

Dog Doghouse Flowers Gate

Can you spot the puppy?

In the farmshop

What are the differences between these two potted plants?

Plant pots

Tomato plant

Cucumber

Bell

Bananas

Wool